This Walker book belongs to:

_____

_____

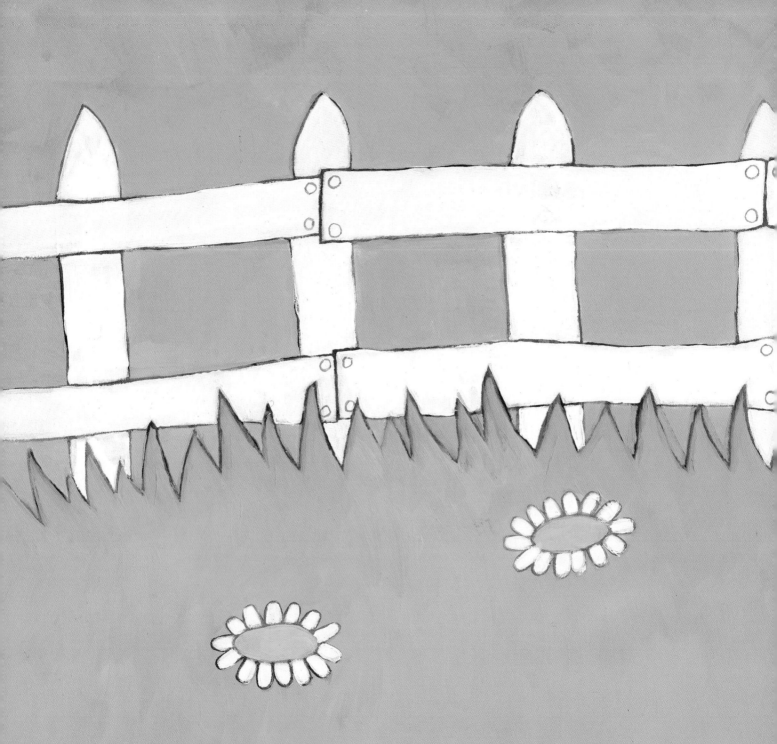

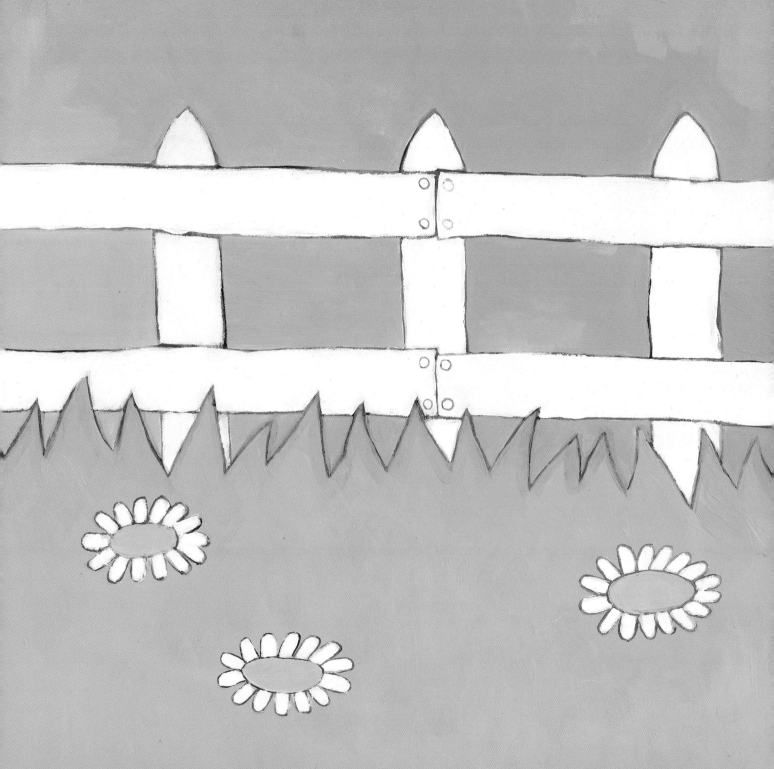

To Ralph (hatched 15.12.94)
T.M.

For Ted
J.C.

First published 1996 by Walker Books Ltd
87 Vauxhall Walk, London SE11 5HJ

This edition published 2008

2 4 6 8 10 9 7 5 3 1

Text © 1996 Tony Mitton

Illustrations © 1996 Jane Chapman

Printed in China

British Library Cataloguing in Publication Data: a catalogue
record for this book is available from the British Library.

ISBN 978-1-4063-1678-0

www.walkerbooks.co.uk

Where's My Egg?

Tony Mitton Jane Chapman

WALKER BOOKS

AND SUBSIDIARIES

LONDON · BOSTON · SYDNEY · AUCKLAND

"I've lost my egg,"
clucks Mama Hen.

"It's not in here,"
barks big dog Ben.

"Is it there in
Puss's bed?"

"Miaow," purrs Puss
and shakes her head.

"Is it tucked in
Donkey's straw?"

"No, it's not!"
squeaks Mrs Mouse.

"Is my egg here,
Mother Duck?"

"These are mine,"
she quacks. "Bad luck."

"Oh dear," clucks Hen. "Where can it be?"

"Hello," cheeps Chick.
"I've hatched...
It's me!"

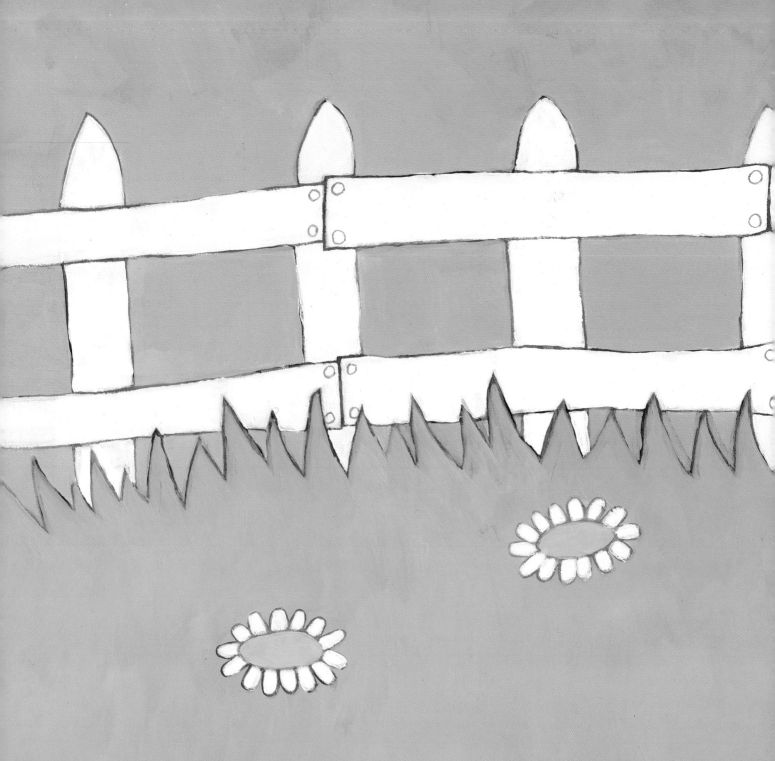

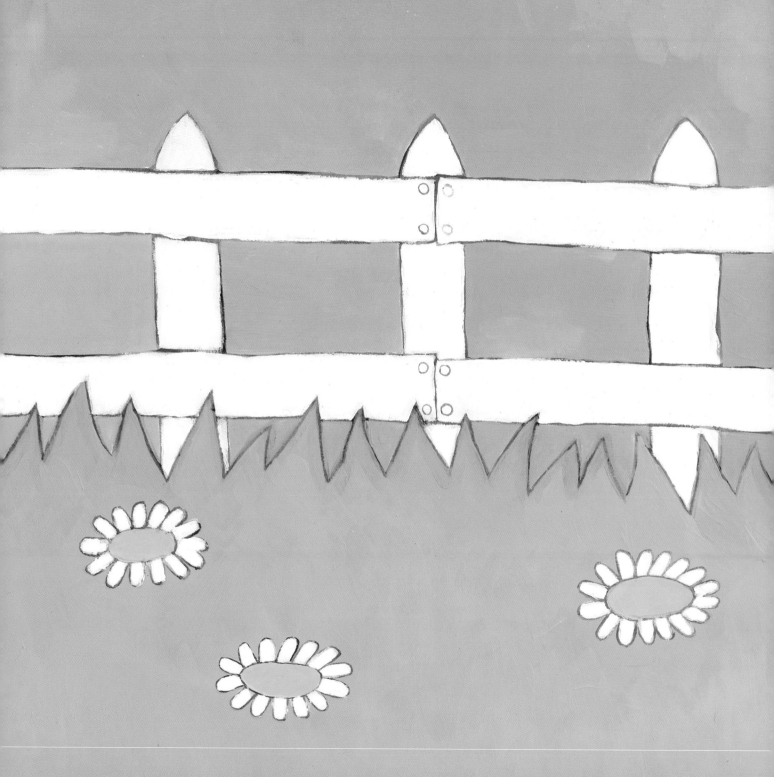